FOLLOW THE LEADER

By Sandy Damashek
Illustrated by Tom Cooke

A SESAME STREET/READER'S DIGEST KIDS BOOK

Published by Reader's Digest Young Families, Inc.,
in cooperation with Children's Television Workshop

"Hey, Bert, let's play follow the leader," said Ernie as he ran down the steps of 123 Sesame Street.

Bert shook his head. "Not now, Ernie," he said. "I'm on my way to the library. I don't have time to play a game."

"Gee, Bert," said Ernie, "I know a shortcut to the library. If you follow me, you'll get there in no time!"

in front of

Ernie and Bert met Grover
in front of Hooper's Store.

behind

"Where are you going?" asked Grover.
"We're going to the library," answered Bert.
"Do you want to come with us, Grover? Just walk
behind Bert," said Ernie.

over

"**Over** we go!" said Ernie as he jumped **over** a fire hydrant.

"**Over** we go," said Grover.

"**Over** we go," said Bert. They jumped **over** the fire hydrant, too.

under

"Now let's go **under** here," called
Ernie. He crawled **under** a big bush next
to the sidewalk.

"Ernie, are you sure you know where
you are going?" asked Bert.

"Just follow me, Bert," said Ernie.
"This is my shortcut."

in

They walked down another street. Suddenly Ernie stopped. "Hmm. Here's the bakery. Let's go **in**," he said.

So the three went **in**.

Four came **out**.
"How did you know where to find me?"
asked Cookie Monster.

between

Next Ernie and Bert and Grover and
Cookie Monster walked **between** two houses . . .

and cut **across** a backyard.

through

"Which way to the library, Ernie?" asked Bert.

"This way, Bert," said Ernie as he climbed **through** a hole in a fence.

Bert followed Ernie **through** the hole in the fence. Then Grover followed Bert.

Cookie Monster followed Grover **through** the hole in the fence—almost.

"Cowabunga!" he cried. He was stuck.

"Oh, my goodness!" said Grover. "We will pull you out!"

So they pulled and pulled until . . . THWUMP! . . . Cookie Monster was free.

Then Ernie led everybody into the playground. Big Bird was waiting for them.

"Hello, everybody!" he said. "I've been watching you. You jumped over the fire hydrant, crawled under the bush, went into the bakery and out of the bakery, walked between two houses and across a backyard, and then you climbed through a hole in the fence. Are you playing follow the leader?"

"No," said Bert. "We're going to the library."

"Well," said Ernie, "we're going to the library—and we're playing follow the leader, too. Do you want to play?"

top

Bert and Grover and Cookie Monster and Big Bird followed Ernie to the **top** of the jungle gym.

bottom

"Let's try the slide next,"
Ernie said.
   So they all slid to the
bottom of the slide.

around

"Come on!" called Ernie, running out of
the playground. "Let's ride on the carousel."
Each one jumped on a different horse and rode
around and **around**.

up

"Let's go!" called Ernie when the carousel
had stopped. He led his friends **up** a big hill.

down

He led his friends **down** the big hill.

near

Then they stopped to rest **near** a boat pond. "Ernie," said Bert, as soon as he had caught his breath, "when are we going to get to the library?"

far

"It won't be long now," said Ernie. "Look."
Far away, they could see a busy city street.
"Follow me," said Ernie.

"Well, Bert, here we are!" said Ernie.

"Oh, neato! The library. Okay, everybody, follow me!" said Bert.

So Bert and Grover and Cookie Monster and Big Bird and Ernie climbed up the steps to the library.

"Hey, Bert. Wait until you see the shortcut I have for the way home!" called Ernie.